Illustrations © 1985 by Roberto Innocenti
Editors: Etienne Delessert, Ann Redpath
Jacket design: Rita Marshall
English translation: Martha Coventry and Richard Graglia.

Published by Creative Editions
123 South Broad Street, Mankato, Minnesota 56001, USA.
Creative Editions is an imprint of The Creative Company

Library of Congress Cataloging-in-Publication Data
Innocenti, Roberto. Rose Blanche / Roberto Innocenti
and Christophe Gallaz.
Summary: During World War II, a young German girl's
curiosity leads her to discover something far more terrible than
the day-to-day hardships and privations that she and her
neighbors have experienced.
ISBN 978-1-56846-189-2
1. World War, 1939-1945—Germany—Juvenile fiction. [1. World
War, 1939-1945—Germany—Fiction. 2. Concentration camps—
Germany—Fiction. 3. War—Fiction. 4. Conduct of life—Fiction.]
I. Gallaz, Christophe, 1948- . II. Title.
PZ7.I586Ro 1996   [Fic]—dc20   95-45378

E F G H

ROSE BLANCHE

ROBERTO ～ INNOCENTI

TEXT BY CHRISTOPHE GALLAZ
AND ROBERTO INNOCENTI

CREATIVE EDITIONS
MANKATO, MINNESOTA

My name is Rose Blanche.
I live in a small town in Germany with narrow streets,
old fountains and tall houses with pigeons on the roofs.
One day the first truck arrived and many men left.
They were dressed as soldiers.
Winter was beginning.

Now the trucks follow each other under the school windows. They are full of soldiers we don't know, but they wink at us.

They drive tanks that make sparks on the cobblestones. They are so noisy and smell like diesel oil. They hurt my ears and I have to hold my nose when they pass by.

Sometimes it seems things haven't really changed.
But my mother wants me to be careful crossing the
street between all the trucks. She says soldiers won't
slow down.

Lots of times I walk by the river, just looking at it.
Branches float along and sometimes old, broken toys.
I like the color of the river. It looks like the sky.

The trucks are fun to watch. We stand in the doorway as they pass. We don't know where they're going. But we think they're going someplace on the other side of the river.

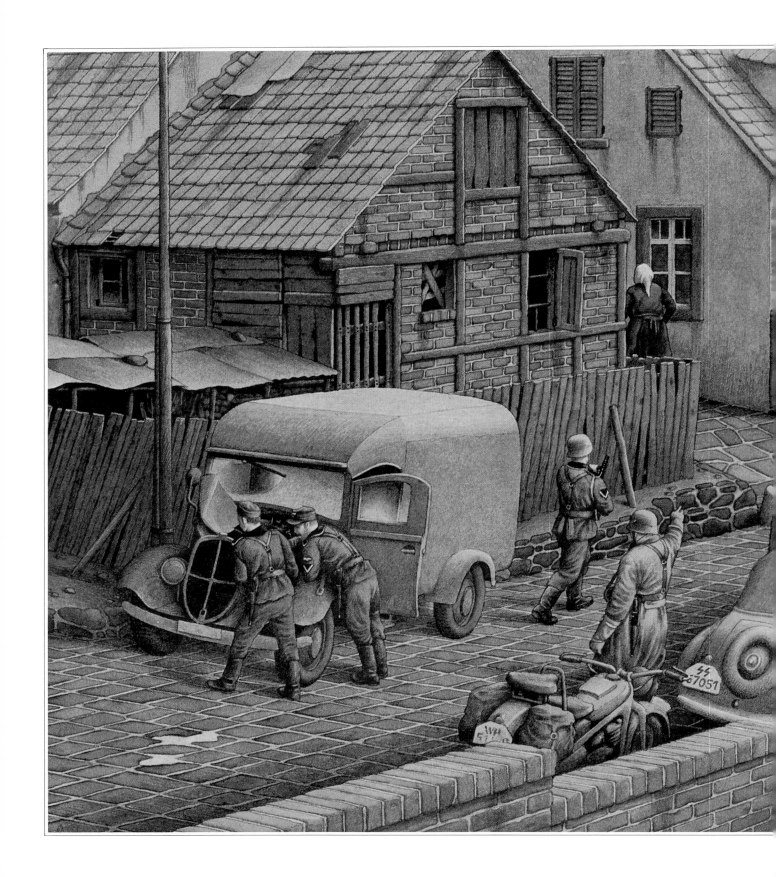

One day one of them stopped so the soldiers could repair the engine. A little boy jumped from the back of the truck and tried to run away. But the mayor was standing there in the middle of the street.

He grabbed the little boy by the collar and brought
him back to the truck. Then he smiled at the soldiers
without speaking. And they thanked him.
　　　The sky was gray.

The soldiers climbed back into the truck; doors
banged shut and it pulled away.
It happened very fast.

I wanted to know where the little boy went. So I watched the truck until it disappeared around the corner. The street was crowded. Kids were playing. There were bicycles and farmer's tractors all over. It was noisy just like every day when school is out. But I walked on the sidewalk ignoring everyone—and no one saw me.

I walked for a long time, past the edge of town into the open fields, where I had never been. The clouds were gray. Everything was frozen. Sometimes I ran.

I followed the tracks into the forest and found
a clearing.

Suddenly, electric barbed wire stopped me.
Behind it there were some children standing still.
I didn't know any of them. The youngest said they
were hungry. Since I had a piece of bread, I carefully
handed it to them through the pointed wires.

They all stood in front of long wooden houses.
The sun was setting behind the hills. It was windy.
I was cold.

Weeks passed by in the pale winter. Rose Blanche's appetite surprised her mother: she took more to school than she ate at home. All the bread and butter she could carry; even more jam and apples from the cellar.

Rose Blanche was getting thinner. In town, only the mayor was staying fat.

Everyone watched everyone else.

Rose Blanche hid her food in her school bag and sneaked out of school early.

By now she knew the road by heart. There were more children by the wooden houses, and they were also getting thinner behind the barbed wire fence. Some of them had a star pinned on their shirts. It was bright yellow.

When the snow melted and the streets were very muddy, the trucks full of weary soldiers drove only at night. This time in the other direction. They were coming with no lights on from the far side of the river, and they never stopped.

One morning all the people of the town fled, carrying pots and burlap bags and chairs. There were soldiers among them. Some had torn uniforms.

Some were limping. Some were in pain
and asking for water.
Rose Blanche disappeared that day.
She had walked into the forest again.

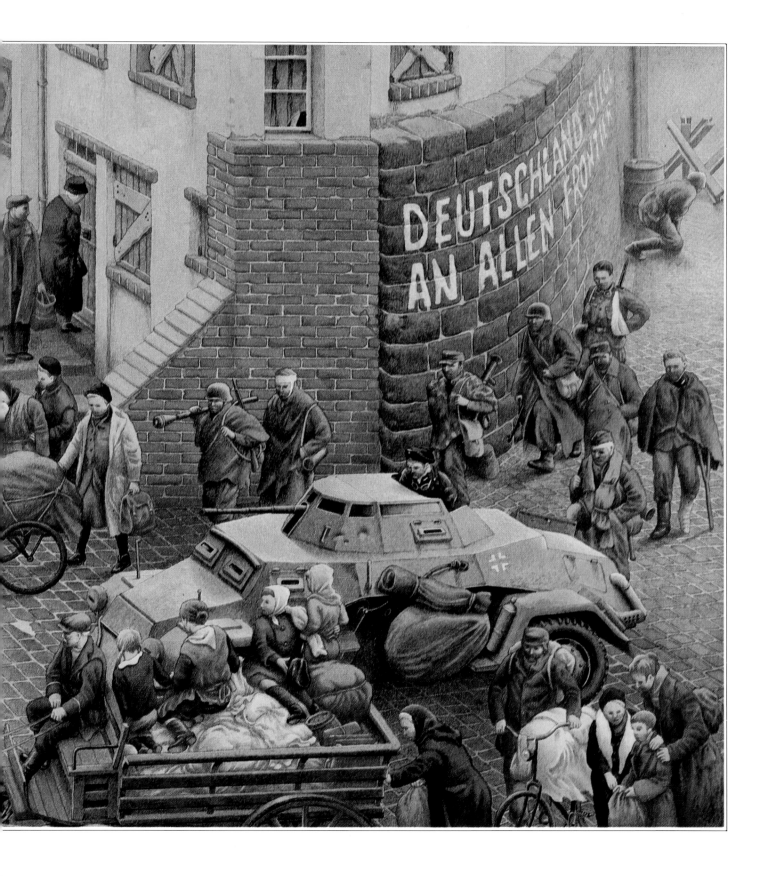

Fog had erased the road. Rose Blanche was hopping around the mud puddles to keep her shoes clean.

In the middle of the woods, the clearing had changed. It was empty. Rose Blanche dropped her school bag full of food. She stood still.

Shadows were moving between the trees. It was hard to see them. Soldiers saw the enemy everywhere.

There was a shot.

At that moment in town, some other soldiers arrived. Their trucks and their tanks were also noisy, and they smelled like diesel oil. But their uniforms were a different color. And they spoke a different language.

Rose Blanche's mother waited a long time for her little girl.

The crocuses finally sprang up from the ground. The river swelled and overflowed its banks. Trees were green and full of birds.

Spring sang.